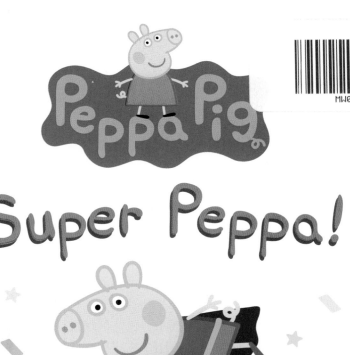

Super Peppa!

Adapted by Lauren Holowaty and Cala Spinner

This book is based on the TV series *Peppa Pig*. *Peppa Pig* is created by Neville Astley and Mark Baker.
PEPPA PIG and all related trademarks and characters TM & © 2003 Astley Baker Davies Ltd/Entertainment One UK Limited.
HASBRO and all related logos and trademarks TM & © 2021 Hasbro. All Rights Reserved. Used with Permission.

ISBN 978-1-338-68105-5

10 9 8 7 6 5 4 3 2 1
Printed in the U.S.A.

21 22 23 24 25
40

First printing 2021

www.peppapig.com

SCHOLASTIC INC.

There's a surprise visitor at Peppa's play group today.
It's Super Potato!

"By the power of vegetables, I am here!" shouts Super Potato.

"Wow!" Peppa says. She loves Super Potato.

Super Potato has lots of amazing powers. Candy Cat wants to know how he can run so fast.

"That's a good question. I would say from eating Brussels sprouts," Super Potato replies.

Super Potato can also fly. He uses his cape to soar through the skies.
Peppa loves to watch Super Potato on television.

At home, Peppa can't stop talking about Super Potato. She thinks he's the coolest visitor ever!

"When I grow up, I want to be super, just like Super Potato," Peppa tells Mummy Pig.

"Hmm," Mummy Pig replies. She gets an idea!

Mummy takes Peppa to Daddy Pig's muddy puddle jumping competition. Daddy Pig leaps up high into the air and lands with a perfect splash!

"Wow, Daddy!" Peppa cries. "You're a super muddy puddle jumper!"

Peppa thinks that jumping high is definitely a superpower!

Peppa leaps high into the air and makes a big splash!
The crowd gets covered in mud and they cheer.

Next, Peppa visits Miss Rabbit. She follows Miss Rabbit from one task to the next.

They race from the supermarket . . .

to the fire station . . .

to the museum . . .

and then to the
movie theater.

After that, Miss Rabbit
takes some visitors for a
helicopter ride . . .

and she and
Peppa give
everyone yummy
ice-cream cones!

"Wow, Miss Rabbit! You're super at everything," Peppa says, as Miss Rabbit drives everyone home on the train.

"If you work hard, you can be super at anything," says Miss Rabbit.

But back at home, Peppa is worried.
"Daddy Pig is super at jumping, and Miss Rabbit is super at so many things," Peppa says. "But I don't feel super at anything. Maybe I'll never be a superhero."

"Being super isn't just about having superpowers," says Mummy Pig. "Today, you gave everyone ice cream and spent time with Daddy Pig. You made everyone happy. That's what being super is about!"

Mummy Pig is right! Peppa might not be able to fly or run fast, but she can always try her best, work hard, and do nice things for others.

The next day at play group, Peppa shows up in a superhero costume.

"I'm not a superhero," says Peppa.
"But I am super. Super Peppa!"

All the other children want to be super just like Peppa. So, she helps them do super things, like play with one another and share toys.

"Every day, we can be a little more super," Peppa says. "We just need to practice and try really hard!"

The children cheer. They love being super. Everyone loves being **Super!**

Be Super, Just Like Peppa!

We can't all have superpowers like Super Potato. But each one of us can be super! Here are some ideas to be super, just like Peppa and her friends.

- Eat lots of leafy vegetables and fruit
- Speak up for those in need
- Spend time with your family and friends
- Share your toys and books
- Say "thank you" when someone does something nice
- Tell someone you love them